the beach

the beach

a collection of poems from my rebirth

jayde lily

dedicated to all those who dared to be different
and understood the loneliness
that would be a byproduct
of their peace.

the warm sand
the ice-cold water
the sky of never-ending lights
deep blues and bright pinks
dancing lavenders and scattered crystals
here I am free
here I am whole.

I feel the same way today as I did when I first looked into your eyes. I remember not being able to breathe. I felt lost in you and found in me. I couldn't stop thinking about you. those eyes. your smile. I felt my body go hot then cold like my soul was being pulled from its vessel. my fingers tingled and my mind whirred. I felt everything and nothing. nothing else mattered. I was stuck in that moment. no chance of being saved. no chance of snapping back to reality. no chance of being who I once was. I feel the same way today as I did back then because you told me that's how you felt about her.

you said that I was perfect
but why did you leave
you looked into my eyes and smiled
but you never looked back
you acted like you didn't want to leave
but you've been gone for a year
now when I hear the word perfect
I can't help but think of you.

jayde lily

this was wonderful
I can't wait to take you on a real date

a year has gone by
and I'm still waiting for you.

jayde lily

I haven't breathed
since you left.

jayde lily

I get morning sickness
because I wake up
and you aren't there.

jayde lily

in another life
I think we would be together
but in this one
I have to see you be happy
without me.

jayde lily

who knew the silence
would be deafening
who knew the hurt
would feel like nothing
who knew that your eyes
would make me feel everything.

jayde lily

after every piece that I write
after every experience shared
I feel cold and weak
like a ghost walked through me
ghosts from my past
leaving
finding new homes
somewhere
I don't have the space anymore
but how many times will I go cold

jayde lily

soul cries
from broken soul ties.

jayde lily

I've fallen in love a thousand times
all because I looked into your eyes
make it a thousand and one
addicted to your smile
the feeling sets my heart ablaze
I've fallen in love a thousand times
and I don't think I can stop
I'm lost in you.

jayde lily

sometimes
I can hear the beach
calling my name
persistent yet soft.

I am earth
fresh mud from the spring rain
wet sand on the beaches of senegal
do you see the generations of pain
the times I was disappointed again and again
I will be constant and always there
I will sprout beauty from our storms
showing you the capacity that I have to care
I am constant and always there
you are the sky
so vast and marvelous
intangible yet you move the trees
like waves crashing
powerful
I'm lost at sea
what secrets are kept in your ethereal blues
do you share my aspirations in life
do you dream in water-colored hues
can you move to my rhythm and sing to my blues
I want to know more
but I should leave well enough alone
back from the sands of time
I blink
and you're gone.

jayde lily

illusions and delusions
of what is and could be
waiting for you to realize
to kiss your brow good morning
to hold me as I sleep
the air depletes when I look into your eyes
hellos and goodbyes
when will you realize
smiling with my eyes
finding ways to say the most mundane things
posing questions as an excuse to get lost in your eyes
lost in hopes I see and discover everything
do you see anything
those eyes are so pretty and blind
impervious to beauty
what do they see at sunset
when fire meets rain
streaks of lavender and orange
beauty and pain
we complement each other
lightning and thunder
sun and moon
fire and rain
those eyes are so full but there is nothing there
no us
no we
no meant to be
you're here
I'm there
you don't
I care
if only those eyes
could see me.

                    jayde lily

the hard part of truth
is that there is no amount
of avoiding ignoring or performing
that will stop the inevitable time
when you must sit with it
and accept it
only then can you move on.

jayde lily

I never pray
but I tried to pray you away.

jayde lily

I woke up
but part of me wishes
I didn't.

jayde lily

I've seen this look before
the anticipation in his eyes
he doesn't want to leave
but he can't bring himself to ask
if he can stay longer
he is waiting for me to say something
other than goodbye
everything is still
the air seems to leave
what do you want to say

I'll never forget the look in his eyes.

jayde lily

when
will I no longer
wake up in a panic
wondering if you're okay
when

jayde lily

thinking of you
is the worst part of my day.

jayde lily

when will the emptiness
go away
because I long for the beach.

how are you
you were on my mind

read yesterday.

jayde lily

I want to say
that I hate you
but I really hate myself
because I fell for you.

jayde lily

I thought you just needed time
but you were just being nice.

jayde lily

I can't stand to look in your eyes
because I can see the pity
I can hear your apathetic tone
I can see your pedestal.

jayde lily

I don't know what else to say
just leave me alone
and get out of my thoughts.

jayde lily

you led me on

...and I'd still follow.

jayde lily

I can usually see red flags
but I ignore them
the mistake I made with you
is that I thought you were
perfect.

jayde lily

I remember talking about our life together
the house in the suburbs
I wanted a big dog
but you wanted a little one
you explored by body
I explored your heart
I wiped the tears from your cheek
and told you that I'd take care of you
I saw your soul
and shed a tear with you
you said that you would try
and I promised to be patient
you disappeared and I was left waiting
but I hope you still find comfort
in the piece of myself I let you have
consider it an everlasting promise
that piece will take care of you always
that look in my eyes
my soft smile
let it bring you warmth
let it tell you that you are worth
every ounce of love you are afraid of
I tried desperately to get you to see that
you tried to look away
but I held your face
you didn't want to be seen
but you needed to be loved
you were afraid
they always are
that I would truly see
all of you
in just a blink
dwell in your essence
care for your heart

jayde lily

protect your peace
challenge your mind
and invigorate your soul
there is nothing you could tell me
to make me go back on my promise
you hurt me
but you still have that piece
of me
the promise that I've got you
and you'll always have me.

you told me that you'd be
my chauffeur
taking me everywhere I wanted or needed
I tried waiting for you to drive me through life
I'd pick the music
you'd hold my leg
I'd kiss your hand at the stop signs
you'd kiss my lips at the red lights
I joked that we'd never make it anywhere
we would be pulled over
hands running through your hair
needing you like air
I guess I was kind of right
because I kept coming downstairs to meet you
but you were never there.

jayde lily

when you told me about her
I started to say goodbye
goodbye to all the tomorrows
all the dates I planned for somedays
the car rides through the city
goodbye to your laugh
your eyes that see me
goodbye to the intimacy
that I was excited to explore
and hello to us no more.

jayde lily

the person who makes you forget
about the beach
is the one who packs your bags
when they hurt you.

how can I be okay one moment
then on edge the next
breathe.

jayde lily

just talk to me
tell me it will be alright.

jayde lily

help…

please.

I'm in the middle
of wanting to try
and wanting to die.

jayde lily

I lie to myself
that you can feel my absence
but I know
that you will never notice.

jayde lily

once again…
I think of that beach.

jayde lily

I had a dream about you
when I woke up I was in panic
because I remembered you weren't there.

jayde lily

I can't tell if I miss you more or less
with each tear
why do I miss you
when I never really had you

jayde lily

I can have your mind
I can have your body
but I'll never have your heart

I'm not allowed.

jayde lily

I went to bed happy
realizing that I deserved a better man than you
I woke up sad
realizing that you would never hold me.

jayde lily

I'm wide awake because
I wish I was sleeping with you
I can't get comfortable
because I should be
lying on your chest
my mind is running
because I didn't get a kiss
to make everything slow
if you were holding me right now
I know I'd be fast asleep
and not up wishing that tonight
would hurry and end.

jayde lily

I feel empty
and I understand why
I've poured into you
with nothing in return
I wondered how you slept
hoped you made it home safe
I've wished you the best days
and prayed you smile
and feel love always
I'm empty
and I wish I knew why
I wasn't good enough
for you to pour into me
love and desire.

jayde lily

I'm not hurt
because of what you did
I'm hurt because
I betrayed myself
by thinking I read you
and your intentions
accurately.

jayde lily

I don't need your pity
I want connection
don't offer out of sympathy
come to me and ask me
how can i show my support
how can i show up
how can i let you know how much i value you
pity only brings out the fire
that is my raging resilience
I've been on the floor before
and I picked myself up
wiped the tears from my cheeks
and continued to be me
so I don't need your pity
or for you to try to fill a spot
because
when I will need you there
you'll be nowhere
so learn me and be direct
and leave your pity for someone else.

jayde lily

my favorite memory of you
is when you sat me down
and told me you couldn't do this
you couldn't continue seeing me
you dictated to me what my body needed
and how my body wanted to be touched
and you left me because you couldn't be that
you disqualified yourself
before you were even in the running
I guess things work out for a reason
because I laugh at the thought
of ever letting you in my bed.

jayde lily

I bought a one-way ticket
to the beach
I hope my grandmother is there.

I'm fine until I think of your eyes
then I am back at one
getting lost in you
and wishing that I wasn't
I wish that I could just leave this life
I'm so tired
I need a break
I need my thoughts to be my own
I need my tears to flow again
I just need
but I'm not allowed
to need.

jayde lily

I'm in the middle of being over you
and wanting you so bad
of realizing I am too good for you
but would take you if you chose me
of being healed
and thinking of you first when I wake up
of having fulfilling days
and lonely nights
when will I stop being lost
in the middle of you.

jayde lily

I realized just how much
I tried to accommodate you
from reaching out
and planning hangouts
to keeping in touch
though it was clear I needed too much
to making excuses
when all my friends
tried to get me to see
that you'd never understand
and that I would never
be a priority.

jayde lily

I don't need pity
I don't need to be empowered
I don't need advice and
I don't need to be spoken for
I need to feel protected
I need to feel valued
I need to feel seen
I need to feel safe.

jayde lily

isn't it funny
how I used to want you so bad
now…
I'd be fine never seeing you again
and forgetting you ever existed.

jayde lily

I was the best thing
that could have happened for you
now you have to live
with that decision.

jayde lily

no matter how many times
you try to replicate
you try to substitute
you try to d-i-y
she will never be me
understand that
and live with it.

jayde lily

part of me is still bitter
that you chose someone else
part of me still hates you
for making me feel it was all in my head
though I want to be back to normal
I don't think I have it in me
I would ask for some space
but that would mean at one point
you were near.

jayde lily

I'm giving myself time
to get over this hurt
but how long do I have to wait
it's felt like forever.

jayde lily

I don't say your name anymore
though once I couldn't stop talking about you
hopefully soon it won't be a reminder
it will just be a name.

jayde lily

it's funny how after talking to others
everyone thinks you are living a lie
no one thinks you're authentic
no one thinks you're as great
as you try to seem
that is a sad reality.

                              jayde lily

always an advocate
but never protected
they say my value is precious
but I go neglected
I only know heartbreak
from time and time again
of mistaking opportunity for love
and a boy for a man.

jayde lily

you say that
I should be empowered
but my true power
would scare you.

jayde lily

what do I write
when there is nothing
left to say
let's just sit in silence
then go our separate ways.

jayde lily

I've come to understand
that part of rebirth
is being okay with doing things alone
learning to breathe on my own
learning to think on my own
going to restaurants
and saying table for one
because I'm there to celebrate
all alone
trying new things on my own
working through my problems
weighing pros and cons
alone
taking long walks
all on my own
not waiting to be validated
because I'm worthy enough
on my own
learning the hard lesson
that since I died alone
I have to be reborn
on my own.

jayde lily

I know I've moved on
when hearing your name
does nothing to me

I'm not there yet.

jayde lily

with every hurt and disappointment
I get closer to the beach
intentional or not I inch forward
but my resilience deepens
it doesn't mean that the beach is gone
I can just smell the water without diving in
I can dip my toes in the warm sand
let the mist of the tide wet my hair
with every hurt I get closer to the beach
I'm not sure I want saving
maybe the beach is where I belong
maybe this will be it
what takes me home
to the beach of the great beyond.

jayde lily

finding peace
is being able to breathe
however
being able to smile
means that I am healing.

jayde lily

I've always wondered
why I have trouble with my femininity
alone my voice soars with emotion and passion
my mannerisms effervescent and soft
why only alone
because alone I am safe
I desire the protection
that allows me to explore
my divine femininity.

jayde lily

I am striving to find peace
in the unease
to remain calm
in the ambiguity
I don't know what is going on
but I know where I'm going
learning not everything
is black and white
and that by trusting my gut
no matter the unease
I will have peace.

jayde lily

I can finally wake up
look in the mirror
and say
good morning beautiful

that is progress.

jayde lily

you've never looked happier
I've never looked into your eyes this much
your hips sway when you walk
sometimes you even smile
when you're alone
you look like you're in love
who is she

me... I'm in love with me.

jayde lily

I spend my days alone
meals for one
no calls on my phone
quietly existing
in a place of my own
I was lonely with you
like I was all alone
in love all on my own
waiting for you to call my phone
because I never wanted
to spend my days alone
but here I am
all alone
falling more in love with me
all on my own.

jayde lily

I'm planted
and soon I will grow.

jayde lily

it is hard
but I'm trying to be patient
anything great
is worth waiting for
and will make up
for all the time that
I waited.

jayde lily

instead of crying myself to sleep
I'm trying something new
I end my nights with gratitude
listing each little thing
that made today better
than my lowest day.

jayde lily

some things are truly better
when they go unsaid.

jayde lily

all of the sudden
the air left the room

where do I belong?

jayde lily

if I go to the beach will I be happy there
sand beneath my feet, saltwater in my hair
will I be alone
or will I meet my grandmother
can I hold my baby cousin and laugh with my aunt
will I have someone
or forced to come to terms with what I'd done
the quiet
the silence
waves crashing in my ears
will I feel the things I felt before
can I laugh and cry
or am I as numb as before
part of me loves blue but
can I be hypnotized by lavender
each star in the sky
being one time I hoped to die?

jayde lily

why does it have to be so hard
to just be me
my doubts and insecurities
dim the already dark world around me
one day I just want to
breathe.

jayde lily

I thought about leaving
going somewhere far away
maybe I could start anew
a new identity with no past
cherish me while I'm here
hold me close and don't let go
tell me I'm wonderful
because next week I may be gone
I flirt with the beaches of the great beyond
they call to me often
with nowhere to call home
maybe it is best that I am gone
but while I'm here
pull me in
say you love me
because tomorrow I might be gone.

jayde lily

there is no need to worry
what is for me
will come my way
the future for me
is already mine
I don't have to fight
for good things
because they will fight for me.

jayde lily

it's okay to not know
it is okay
to not know
just do what feels right.

jayde lily

I can feel the threshold
I'm getting more and more
uncomfortable
I feel the pressure building
I can see the shell splitting
soon I will shine
sparkle dazzle and glow
I'll be reborn
just beyond this threshold.

jayde lily

I know a place where I can be free.

I am helplessly
irrevocably
and utterly in love
with me

at least that is what I will say
until it is true.

jayde lily

a glass of chardonnay
narrowed eyes
I lean in

how did you get here

jayde lily

I am light
I am love
I am precious.

jayde lily

where do I go now
I feel happily lost.

jayde lily

when did you get here
have I seen you before
your eyes are…captivating
I've never seen someone so stunning
it's like you know me
like we were meant to be
or like I knew you in another life
I don't know how to say this but
I already know that you're the one
because I am you
and you are me.

jayde lily

I used to never look into the mirror
now I can't stop smiling when I do.

jayde lily

she is made from love
but has never felt it
it shines from her seams
it beams from her eyes
effervescence is her name
ephemeral being to be adored
she walks with confidence
because she knows what it is to be ignored
she's heard it all before
perfection incarnated
yet she still walks alone
those who have tried
can't keep up
those who can't
try to trip her up
she's made of love
to be protected by grace
to be in her presence is a gift
to be loved by her is transformative
when she shows her grays and rainy days
you'll be stunned to see her beams
sunlight through the clouds
bringing color to your dreams
she is love
by way of grace.

jayde lily

this is the last thing I'm writing
I have nothing left
and I don't know
how to say it
or make you understand
or get you to feel it
in the place you hide
from everyone.
I want you
I really want you
not the version of you
that you show
I want the version of you
that you don't
I feel peace when I think of you
like a saturday morning rain
birds chirping
and the leaves rustling
I looked in your eyes
and said I do
the very first time we met
you don't know it
but I'm already yours
I've seen you buy the ring
I've seen you buy the house
I've seen the look of fear
when you say something
that hurts me
for the first and only time
I've prayed you away
I've deleted your contact
I said you were worthless
and made my friends hate you
all to get rid of you

jayde lily

why won't you fucking leave
why are you the first
and last thing on my mind
why do I dream about you
about us
just leave me alone
I hate that I met you
and looked into those eyes
but I wait day and night
for you to be mine
I could imagine a life
without you but
my mind won't let me
hopefully writing this book
is just what I need
to finally be free
from you…

I've consulted the universe
and listened to my divine
I've seen your eyes
look deeply into mine
I feel a deep pull in my chest
like someone is taking my breath
breaths down my neck
pain in my chest
the vibrations won't let me be
your energy reverberating
in me
through me
around me
it consumes me
the only priority
I am never one to need
I only ever depend on me
but at the top of my mind
at the core of my divine
you have something I need
I need to know with absolute clarity
what in you is pulling me
what doesn't let me sleep
what makes me keep pouring
when I've long been empty
I can hear a part of you calling
tell me what it is
so I can have peace
tell me what it is
when you come back to me.

jayde lily

It is an odd feeling
to be tapped into my divine nature
I'm a liminal being
between this realm and the next
between this existence
and whatever may come after
between you and me
between us and we
my chakras align
and I'm no longer blind
I'm reborn in my divine
my divine
the divine
experiencing thoughts and feelings
that aren't familiar like mine
then I feel a pull
it takes my breath away
it causes my physical body pain
they need me
pull
I'm here
pull
you're safe with me
pull
I make space in my divine sanctity
I'm happily lost within my divine
waiting for the next pull
from a heart that isn't mine.

jayde lily

this pen has been my lifeline
this book my therapy
I've learned and grown
healing from the emotional wounds
I can close this chapter
with absolute clarity
and move on with resolve
you pushed me into my destiny
circumstance brought my purpose
I can hear the tide's calm
and smell the ocean breeze
the beach has called my name
I'm going with no fear
sorry to my loved ones on the other side
I'm not done here
I'm finding my beach
on this side
where I'm free
where I'm bold
effervescence by way of grace
iron resilience of my divine
divine femininity and power
I'm on my way to my beach
and finally in love with me.

- to be continued -

jayde lily

to all my inspirers,

thank you for your part in this chapter of my life. from the men who lied to me and left me lonely, to the friends who have made me feel safe without hesitation. I thank the ones who made me feel delusional, and doubt every fiber of my being, and the ones who had little to no regard for my well-being. in this chapter, I have been feared and hurt by the same people. yet, through this lifeline, I have been able to process, purge, and grow. because of you, I enter the next chapter of my life more resilient and more precious. I am now on my way to *the beach*.

divinely yours,
jayde

the beach is a story of love, loss, and rebirth. I longed for the beach that I'd soon find. my journey of growth kept me here to find love and purpose. alone and in love with me all on my own. on my beach, I'm finally free.

Read a sample of the upcoming release from Jayde Lily,
oceans apart.

oceans apart

finding myself in divine separation

jayde lily

the easiest thing I ever did
was love you
the hardest thing I ever did
was leave you

oceans apart

I've spent my time
drinking my feelings away
dancing my demons out
then dancing with them
I've shown more skin
and made the sweetest friends
what was holding me back?
I have felt so free
I've been so me
I go by Jayde now
I'm no longer
who you've known me to be.

jayde lily

oceans apart

love
beloved
sir
daddy
I will call you whatever
to get you to choke me
and tell me you love me
intoxicated with passion
dive into my waters
deep and crashing
dominate my body
but submit your heart
love me
hard
right now
on this beach.

jayde lily

oceans apart

maybe oceans apart
is where we belong
when we were close
nothing came from it
just delusions that in time
this connection could grow
maybe oceans apart
is where we will stay
maybe one day
the ocean will go away
I search for the right words to say
when the ocean is no longer in my way
maybe just maybe
the ocean is my divine
waiting for me to understand
that you will never
be mine.

jayde lily

oceans apart

I lie on the beach
my skin like melted caramel
the tide is hypnotizing
the sounds of water and palm trees
in the warmth of sun beams
I close my eyes in peace
and open them
to that beautiful lavender sky
crystal stars rain astral dust
like confetti
I glitter in the moonlight
nobody next to mine
I learned to connect and visit
my most divine
if my power can close the gap
between this world and the divine
can it move the oceans
to put your beach next to mine
to see the glimmer in your eye
to be the wind to your sky
can I use my power
to make this union divine.

jayde lily